ublished by Lift Bridge Publishing
opyright© 2021 by Michael Ngbal

brary of Congress Cataloging-in-Publication Data
itle: Chew Chew Spoon

BN 9781637909034
RINTED IN THE UNITED STATES OF AMERICA FIRST EDITION

chew chew spoon

Here comes Chew Chew Spoon

Chewchewchewchewchewwww

Inward, around and straightforward like a handmade motor

Chew Chew Spoon goes into motion. The secret password is open

"Open"

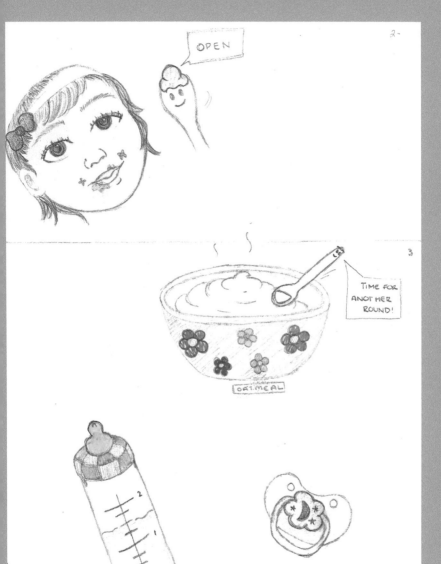

Chew, Chew, aah, Chew, Chew, aah.

Voila!

Chaoum, chaoum, chaoum, Chew Chew

Spoon dips in the station

Time for another round, Chew Chew

Spoon goes into motion

Inward, straightforward like a handmade

motor

The secret password is "open"

Chew chew, aah, chew chew, aah

Chaoum, chaoum, chaoum

Chew chewww. Voila, Chow!

Chew Chew

Spoon!

CPSIA information can be obtained
at www.ICGtesting.com
Printed in the USA
BVHW021712030821
613540BV00001B/8

ublished by Lift Bridge Publishing

opyright© 2021 by Michael Ngbakoua

ibrary of Congress Cataloging-in-Publication Data
itle: Chew Chew Spoon

;BN 9781637909034
RINTED IN THE UNITED STATES OF AMERICA FIRST EDITION

chew chew spoon

Here comes Chew Chew Spoon

Chewchewchewchewchewwww

Inward, around and straightforward like a handmade motor

Chew Chew Spoon goes into motion. The secret password is open

"Open"

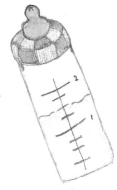

Chew, Chew, aah, Chew, Chew, aah.

Voila!

Chaoum, chaoum, chaoum, Chew Chew

Spoon dips in the station

Time for another round, Chew Chew

Spoon goes into motion

Inward, straightforward like a handmade

motor

The secret password is "open"

Chew chew, aah, chew chew, aah

Chaoum, chaoum, chaoum

Chew chewww. Voila, Chow!

Chew Chew

Spoon!

CPSIA information can be obtained
at www.ICGtesting.com
Printed in the USA
BVHW021712030821
613540BV00001B/8